Wisdom and good-
ness, one at heart;
We never find
them far apart.

AESOP'S
FABLES *in*
RHYME *for*
LITTLE
PHILOSOPHERS

AESOP *the* SLAVE

HE was a slave of Athens long ago;
    A human being, bartered, bought, and sold.
But Aesop's spirit lives through time we know,
    And is a priceless gift unbought by gold.
He gave his wisdom, covered by a cloak
    Of *little stories*, very living parts
Of all the wealth of wisdom that he spoke;
    These live in freedom in our human hearts.

AESOP'S FABLES IN RHYME

for Little Philosophers

by

JOHN MARTIN

Illustrated by
George L. Carlson
and W. Fletcher White

Published by
Dover Publications, Inc.
Mineola, New York

Bibliographical Note

Aesop's Fables in Rhyme for Little Philosophers, first published by
Dover Publications, Inc., in 2014, is an unabridged republication of the
work originally published by John Martin's Book House, New York, in
1924.

Library of Congress Cataloging-in-Publication Data

Martin, John, 1865–1947.
    [Aesop's fables in rhyme for little philosophers]
    Aesop's fables in rhyme / John Martin ; illustrated by George L.
Carlson and W. Fletcher White.
        p. cm.
    "An unabridged republication of the work originally published as
Aesop's Fables in Rhyme for Little Philosophers by John Martin's
Book House, New York, in 1924."
    ISBN-13: 978-0-486-78180-8
    ISBN-10: 0-486-78180-1
      1. Fables, Greek—Adaptations. [1. Stories in rhyme. 2. Fables.]
I. Aesop. II. Carlson, George L., illustrator. III. White, W. Fletcher,
illustrator. IV. Title.
PZ8.3.M363193Ae 2014
[E]—dc23
                                  2014012866

Manufactured in the United States by Courier Corporation
78180101   2014
www.doverpublications.com

DEDICATION
to ALL
of MY CHILDREN

Dear Little Friends:
With happiness
And loving wishes, too,
I hereby give and *dedicate*
This friendly book to you.
There, now it is most surely *yours;*
And its bright pages hold
A hidden store of treasure which
Is better far than gold.
Now, when you read this Fable Book
Just let your spirits reach
Down into deeper meanings that
These old, old stories teach.
I see no reason in the world
Why *children* should not be
As wise philosophers in life
As grown-up folk like me.
That's why I give this book to you.
I *know* you'll look and see
The useful wisdom underneath
Its veiled philosophy.

John·martin

FABLES
THIS BOOK of YOURS INCLUDES

The STAG at the SPRING
A Fable from Aesop

THERE was a stag (so Aesop says)
That wandered through the woodland ways.
He ate the forage of the wood
And found it plenty, sweet and good.

At times he drowsed where shadows creep
'Mid tangled brushes, green and deep;
He seemed content; well might he be,
So sleek and stalwart, safe and free.

Now with all things well satisfied,
A little meadow spot he spied;
Among its shadows, still and cool,
There was a clear and pretty pool.

"Ah," said the stag, "ere sleeping, first
I'll seek to quench my growing thirst."
Across the meadow green he went,
And o'er the silent pool he bent
To take a long, refreshing drink,
Cool from the water's mossy brink.

But *no!* He started up instead
With widened eyes and lofty head.
Reflected in the waters bright
He saw *himself*—a pleasant sight.
He did not drink, but stood quite still
In foolish pride to get his fill
Of looking at his form, for he
Was somewhat spoiled by vanity.

"Ah," said the stag, "to say the least
I am a very handsome beast.
No creature has such horns as mine,
So beautiful, and strong, and fine.
How well they balance, wide they spread
From tip to tip above my head.
If *only* all the rest of me
Were half so splendid, I should be
The envy of the forest wide,
And mayhap all the world beside.
But oh, alas, *those legs of mine!*
Behold their thin and shapeless line.
I am ashamed to look and see
Such graceless things a part of me."

Scarce had he spoken his last word
Than he in stricken panic heard
The very worst of forest sounds—
The bay of swift pursuing hounds.

Quick as the light, off sped the stag
O'er open places, moor and crag.
The *legs* he so despised bore him
Beyond the reach of danger grim.

But, at the moment when he thought
Himself quite safe his antlers caught
In some thick brushes, holding him
Fast as if tethered limb by limb.

Alas, alack, the *horns* which he
Had so admired proved to be
The very parts of him to lend
The means to his unhappy end.
For, bound and helpless in his shame
The pack of baying hunters came
And bore him down. Thus, dears, you see
The danger of such vanity.

    *   *   *

Yes, let us in our very hearts
Do honor to our humbler parts,
For beauty too much glorified
Is sure to trouble and misguide.

THEN our old man without a word unbound
The wood and gave a stick to every son.
Of course, those boys without an effort found
It easy to break fagots *one by one*.

The OLD MAN and his SONS
A Fable from Aesop

THERE was a man, respected, old, and kind,
   With six big sons who quarreled constantly.
This grieved him sorely, and he sought to find
A way to peace at home—where peace should be.

He tried commands and kindlier appeal;
   He pled respect for age and home and name,
But still they quarreled on and did not feel
   The least regret, nor see the growing shame.

At last the father found a goodly way
   To show their folly and at once to prove
That discord breeds a host of sins that prey
   Upon the works of peace and deeds of love.

At once our good man called his wrangling brood,
 And taking up a bundle of short sticks
Well bound together and of stalwart wood,
 Straight, smooth, and clean, and numbering just six,

"My sons," said he, "I want you each to try
 To *break* those sticks in any way you please.
You have not strength enough, and I defy
 Your brawn to shatter or to splinter these."

Each son in turn tried with his burly might
 To break the bundle, but no jerk nor strain
Could even *bend* the fagots bound so tight;
 No strength availed, all struggle was in vain.

Then our old man without a word unbound
 The wood and gave a stick to every son.
Of course, those boys without an effort found
 It easy to break fagots *one by one*.

"There, sons of mine," the wise old father said,
 "You see the *strength of all united things!*
By quarreling you're weakened and misled,
 And *think* of all the needless pain it brings!

Stay bound together by the bonds of love,
  And naught in life can hurt you and no power
Can meet such might as yours. I pray you, prove
  The truth of this each passing day and hour.
But, sons of mine, *divided* as you are,
  Unloving and unloved in bitter pique,
You wreck your peace, and is it singular
  That you who should be strong are dull and weak?
Oh, sons, let not dissension's spell disarm
  Your manhood lest great evil come to you;
For *easy* it would be to do you harm
  As breaking *unbound, single* sticks in two."

QUARRELS

THERE is no good in quarreling;
  There is no use in it.
A quarrel only hurts our Hearts,
  And doesn't help a bit.

A quarrel is a lot of *words*
  And angry sounds that start
The very worst of feelings in
  The middle of the Heart.

Nobody quarrels if he wants
  To wisely use his wits,
For quarrels muddle up our brains
  In useless little bits.

A quarrel only weakens us
  And wastes good energy
That should be used to make our lives
  More what they *ought* to be.

Let's throw all quarrel *feeling* out,
  You see, it really pays,
Because our *POWER* can be used
  In lots of better ways.

IT SEEMS TO ME

IT seems to me not only wise
But always really well
Just to *forget* what we have heard
That isn't right to *tell*.

It seems to me it's wise to be
Quite careful what we *teach,*
Unless we're very sure that we
Can practice what we preach.

It seems to me, pie up too high
Looks very great and grand;
But I'll not be ambitious with
Two cookies well in hand.

The fox may howl, "Sour grapes!"
When they are out of reach,
But my bread spread with gratitude
Is better than a peach.

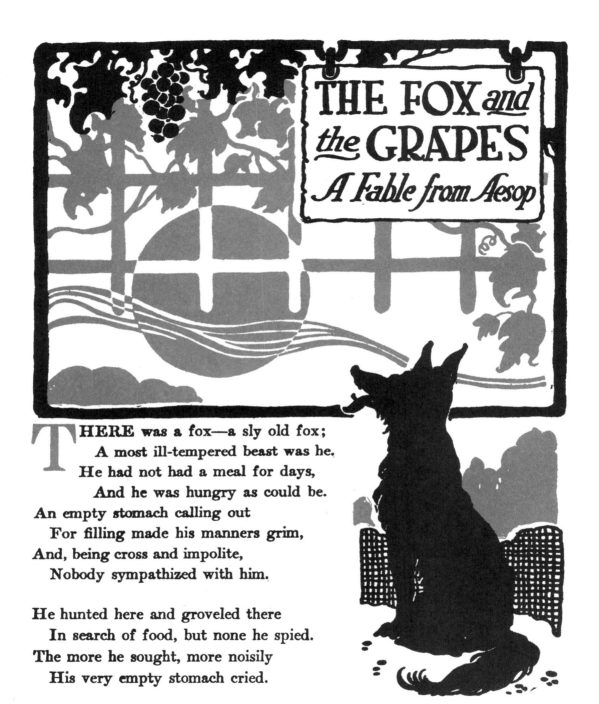

THE FOX and the GRAPES
A Fable from Aesop

THERE was a fox—a sly old fox;
　　A most ill-tempered beast was he.
He had not had a meal for days,
　　And he was hungry as could be.
An empty stomach calling out
　　For filling made his manners grim,
And, being cross and impolite,
　　Nobody sympathized with him.

He hunted here and groveled there
　　In search of food, but none he spied.
The more he sought, more noisily
　　His very empty stomach cried.

At last his staggering footsteps led into a trellised garden where
Grapes hung above his very head in purple clusters ripe and fair.
But they hung high, where sun and air contrived with evening's gentle dew
To give them flavor and sweet bloom. Yes, thus those juicy clusters grew.

"Good food!" cried fox, as up he leaped
  With smothered growlings, rude and gruff.
His two jaws snapped, but never could
  That hungry fox jump high enough.
He leaped again, this way and that,
  In far more ways than I can tell,
And all he got of those fair grapes
  Was but a most far-distant *smell*.

Oh, yes, he was a stalwart fox, with muscles very hard and stout,
But so much jumping, all in vain, soon wore the snapping beastie out,
At last, convinced that juicy meal could not be captured to devour,
He walked away and said,—

"WHO CARES ? It's plain to see those grapes are SOUR"

Ah, foolish fox, we children see
   Into your mean, begrudging speech.
You can't say good words of the things
   You are not big enough to reach.
March on, old fox, perhaps in time
   You'll learn the lesson good taste teaches.
Don't let your own shortcomings force
   You into harsh, unpleasant speeches.

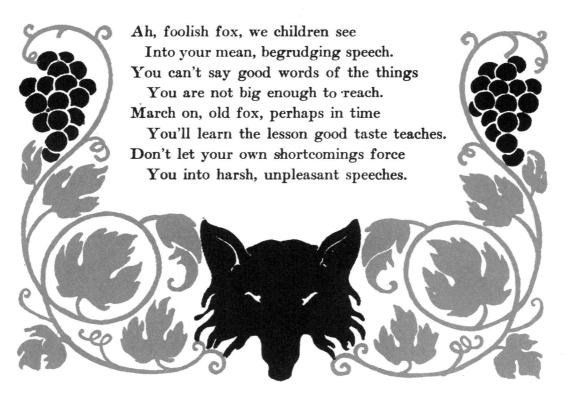

FLOWER SEEDS

A GENTLE word, dropped here and there,
   Is very like a little seed
That grows into a flower fair,
   For troubled hearts that bleed.

A gentle, thoughtful little word,
   May slip into some Heart and bring
The help that heals, and like a bird
   That aching Heart may sing.

Oh, what a garden life might be
   If every day such seeds were sown,
And oh, the happiness when we
   May claim them as our own!

"WITHOUT a tail, joys follow by the score!
My figure? Oh, such gracefulness of line!
I never *half* enjoyed my life before
I lost my tail. Good luck is surely mine."

THE FOX WHO LOST HIS TAIL :
A Fable from Aesop

THERE was a fox; though sly as sly could be
 This did not save him from the sad mishap
 Of losing his fine tail most carelessly
When sitting down too near a thoughtless trap.
When he was well enough to be around,
 He sallied forth to make a little call
Upon some neighbor foxes, and he found
 They didn't sympathize with him at all.
What's more, the neighbors, without mercy, chaffed
 And ridiculed and impolitely teased.
A fox without a tail! Oh, how they laughed!
 Of course, that injured fox was much displeased.

He didn't like such treatment in the least
 But hid his shame beneath a foxy smile,
And then he thought (the silly, scheming beast),
 "I'll fix the teasers by a little guile.
Watch me persuade these animals to let
 Their tails be cut off, too; this cannot fail
To make us all alike, then they'll forget
 To notice that I've lost my precious tail."

So pleased was he with this most clever plan
    Concocted in his selfish, scheming head,
That off he ran and gathered all the clan
    Of foxy beasts, to whom he slyly said:
"I am *surprised* to see you wearing tails!
    They're not in style, are always in the way.
They weigh enough to make you run like snails.
    Come, cut them off. What earthly use are they?
I wouldn't wear a nuisance that depends
    Upon *my* wits to keep it out of traps.
       Cut off your tails! Be comfortable, my friends;
        Discard such trash with other worthless scraps.
    Without a tail, joys follow by the score!
       My figure? Oh, such gracefulness of line!
    I never *half* enjoyed my life before
       I lost my tail. Good luck is surely mine."

"Hear, hear!" exclaimed the foxes gathered round,
    Who waved their tails and tittered all in chorus,
"Hear, hear! When was such wisdom ever found?
    A tailless prophet surely stands before us."

But wait—for then a sly *old* fox arose.
    That he was wise 'twas very plain to see.
Yes, he was stiff of joint, but his sharp nose
    Was long and gray with guile and dignity.

"See here, young fox," said he, "it seems to me
    You offer us too many bobtailed lures.
Concern about our tails much less would be
    If you were not so much deprived of yours.

"We doubt so much your real and true concern
    That we will keep our tails where tails should be,
For it is said that selfish foxes yearn
    For company to share their misery."

SYMPATHY

THAT word *sympathy;* a good word to hear;
When honest and tender, how blessed and dear!
And what does it mean? Not just what is *heard.*
And what is its value? Not merely a *word.*
True sympathy glows with love from the heart;
With things cold and selfish it carries no part,
It asks no reward; in serving it lives;
In loving concern it ungrudgingly gives.
Not pitiful words, nor quick-falling tears,
Not thoughtless expressions of evil and fears.
No—true sympathy goes not by the road
Of *keeping* the trouble or bearing the load;
But from its own faith it asks us to share
The knowledge that we are in God's constant care.
It sees as we see, and feels as we feel,
But *thinking* as love it hastens to heal.

True sympathy is a balm to the soul
Its *love,* ever living, makes perfect and whole.

THE CAT AND THE BIRDS
AN AESOP FABLE IN RHYME

ONE morning in May,
    Or maybe in June,
      The old **rascal** Tom—
        Old Thomas, the cat,
Dressed up to look like
    A doctor and he
      Just fitted the part
        With pills and high hat.

With great dignity and whiskers profound,
    He licked off his smile, and winked out a tear,
And went forth to call on birds in a cage—
    Such *nice* little birds who chanced to live near.

    "Good morning," said **he**,
      "I heard you **were** ill.
        My heart **aches** for **you**;
          I've hurried to **see**
    If I could help you
      Or **serve** you and yours.
        Command me, I pray.
          (Don't mention the fee.)"

To hear Doctor Tom
 Express sympathy
  Would soften the heart
   Of a stone, good and quick.
To look at his *eye*,
 His tearful old eye,
  Would make any one
   Quite *glad* to be sick.

But the birdies just winked, and then winked again
 And said, "Many thanks, but you've come in vain.
We're perfectly well.   See how we can wink.
 We can't rake or scrape an ache or a pain.

"We're quite well, indeed,
 And so shall remain.
  The door's locked *inside*,
   The key's on the shelf.
Good-bye, Doctor Tom,
 Go look in the glass
  And wink all the winks
   You can wink at yourself."

SONG

WHEN things don't go quite right,
  Like washing dirty faces;
When toys and books and dolls
  Are never in their places;
When all goes wrong with everything,
  We SING—SING—SING.

When rainy weather comes
  And many duties press us;
When being good is hard
  And likely to distress us;
When little disappointments *sting,*
  We SING—SING—SING.

There's nothing in the world
  Like pretty music stealing
Into our little hearts
  For happy, wholesome healing.
We clear up all that's going wrong
  With SONG—SONG—SONG.

AND being lads of common sense,
With gratitude a loving pleasure
Each one recalled their father's words
About the hidden treasure.

THE FIELD OF TREASURE

AN AESOP FABLE IN RHYME

A WORTHY farmer knowing that
    His mortal end was drawing near
Desired that his last bequests
    Should be quite plain and clear.

And wishing his three sons to know
    The endless treasure to be won
By honest work, called them and said—
    "My work is nearly done.

"My earthly goods I leave to you,
    And blithely do my old hands yield
This house, my name, and treasure great
    Hid deep in yonder field."

The days passed by; each bringing good
    According to man's wit to measure;
And then the farmer lads began,
    To seek their father's treasure.

With pick and spade and furrow deep
    They dug the field of yielding mould
But found no piece or semblance of
    Their father's hidden gold.

"Whew! That was work!" one lad exclaimed,
  "At least the job we've done is neat;
Now that the field is ploughed and dug,
  We might as well plant wheat."

And so they did exactly that,
  And in due time the good field bore
A crop five times as rich and big
  As ever known before.

And being lads of common sense,
  With gratitude and loving pleasure
Each one recalled their father's words
  About the hidden treasure.

And having wits to match their hearts,
  As well as hands that would not shirk,
They learned that treasure is not *gold*
  But fruit of honest work.

TREASURE

WHEN things don't go exactly right,
   And happy smiles are slow to come;
When, somehow, spirits are not bright
   And satisfied with home—
If we but do a kindly deed,
   Or lift some little weight of care,
Or try to serve some one in need,
   Our pot of gold is there.

When disappointment *hurts* and we
   Think joy will never come again,
When blues are blue as blue can be,
   And ache just like a pain—
If we will think of all the *good*
   God gives His children everywhere,
And fill our hearts with gratitude,
   Our pot of gold is there.

The rainbow is an emblem of
   Good hope, and we can all depend
Upon God's never-failing love
   Down at the rainbow's end.
So, let a rainbow leave the glow
   Of treasure in the *heart,* for where
God's promise is, we surely know
   Our pot of gold is there.

THE DAYS

SOME days are bright
   With light and sun;
Some days are full
   Of joy and fun,
Some days are dark,
   With clouds and rain;
And some days bring
   The sting of pain.
God makes up Time
   By days and days,
And gives them all
   Quite diff'rent ways;
If God should make
   Sun and no rain,
Or endless fun
   Without a pain,
It would be hard
   For us to see
How good the sun
   And health can be,
Yes, days are just
   Like us, for we
All act and live
   Quite diff'rently.

SPILT MILK

WHY mourn about the "might have been's"?
The present joy is best.
Show grateful hearts for what we have,
The dear God does the rest.

Why cry for what we haven't, when
Each blessed, passing minute
Is full of things to make us glad
Of every second in it?

Why whine, or fret for this and that?
Why make a spoiling spot
Upon the lovely things we have?
Oh, we have such a *lot!*

Why let complaint and discontent
Make any shadow-scar
Across the sunshine of the heart
Where all true blessings are?

Spilt milk is spilled. We will not cry,
For crying never sets
A pretty scene for blessings that
The dear God ne'er forgets.

A COUNTRY MAID and her BUCKET of MILK

A FABLE FROM AESOP MADE INTO A MAYTIME SONG

TUM-te-tiddle-ee-tum-ta-ray!
A country maid on the broad highway—
Her cheeks were roses, her hair was gold;
Her lips were cherries, so I've been told.
But a thoughtless maid and a vain was she,
A foolish maid as you soon shall see.
And this was all in the month of May
Tum-te-tiddle-ee-tum-ta-ray!

Tum-te-tiddle-ee-tum-ta-ray!
This country maid was giddy and gay.
A pail of milk on her head she bore,
All fresh and sweet; a gallon or more.
The gallon of milk was hers to sell,
But she was silly, so I've heard tell.
And this was all on a pleasant day.
Tum-te-tiddle-ee-tum-ta-ray!

Tum-te-tiddle-ee-tum-ta-ray!
These are the vanities she did say—
"I'll sell my milk for money and then
I'll buy me eggs and a setting hen.
When they are hatched I'll feed them so
Both big and fat my chickens will grow.
I'll sell them all on a market day."
Tum-te-tiddle-ee-tum-ta-ray!

Tum-te-tiddle-ee-tum-ta-ray!
"The pounds and shillings and pence will pay
For satin shoes and a gown of silk,
A bonnet with feathers as white as milk.
To town, on a market day I'll fare.
At me and my beauty the lads will stare.
But I'll *toss* my head as I turn away."
Tum-te-tiddle-ee-tum-ta-ray!

Tum-te-tiddle-ee-tum-ta-ray!
She *tossed* her head in the month of May.
The milk she bore went *a-splash* alas,
All over the road and the Maytime grass.
Gone were the eggs and the chickens and gown,
Alack! for the jaunt to the market town.
She counted her chickens too soon that day.
Tum-te-tiddle-ee-tum-ta-ray!

The MISGUIDED ASS (AN AESOP FABLE IN RHYME.)

THERE was a donkey beast who said,
  "Why doesn't master cuddle *me*,
  And give me food from his own hand,
  And let me sit upon his knee?

That woolly little dog of his
  Does anything the creature pleases:
The master laughs at barks and wags
  And chuckles when the canine sneezes.
That man's neglect most surely is
  Insulting to a noble ass.
Ha! why should I in silence let
  Such folly uncorrected pass?"

So, donkey beast resolved forthwith
  To imitate the dog and see
How great a household favorite
  An ass with dog-like ways might be.

One day the master settled down
  For solid comfort in his chair,
When in the room the donkey pranced
  With snorts and brays that rent the air.

He gambolled, kicking up his heels;
    He brayed some more with all his might
Until his master nearly died
    With laughter at the funny sight.

Not satisfied with this, the ass
    Got more familiar, if you please,
And put both of his awkward hoofs
    Upon the good man's worthy knees.
He even strove to bark a bit,
    Then, (oh, that *most* misguided chap,)
Proceeded very friskily
    To jump into his master's lap!

"Help!" cried the man, "a joke like this
    Is going just too far, I say.
Help, stable boys, or any one!
    Come, drive this wretched beast away."

MOST thankful was that donkey beast
    At finding that his legs were able
To take him soon and safely to
    His erstwhile home~the donkey stable.

In answer to the lordly call
   The servants gathered by the score
And *whacked* that foolish donkey till
   His feelings and his hide were sore.

Most thankful was that donkey beast
   At finding that his legs were able
To take him soon and safely to
   His erstwhile home —the donkey stable.
Safe in his stall, with lots of hay
   That one-time frisky ass reflected —

"In life we look for certain things
   And then we get the unexpected.
'Tis best, methinks, to be ourselves;
   No masks are good as our own faces;
An ass should always be an ass.
   We all have our respected places."

The WIND and the SUN
A Fable from Aesop

THE Wind can rush and bluster
  And twist and tear and turn;
  The Sun's far-reaching power
Can wilt and parch and burn.
One day, the Wind all prideful
  With mighty blowings blew
Up to the Sun and said, "Sir,
  I'm stronger far than *you!*"
The Sun in burning glory
  Up in his sky so blue,
Said, "Sir, you are mistaken.
  Your statement is not true.
I am by far the stronger
  And I can prove it, too!"
"All right," said Wind, with vigor,
  "If you can prove it—*do.*"
So thus they vainly argued,
  And neither would give in;
At last they made a wager,
  Each thinking he would win.

And this is how they wagered
   (Both chuckling at the joke)—
They'd prove their strength upon a
   Poor trav'ler in a cloak.
The one who proved the stronger,
   And he who won the bet,
Would be the one succeeding
   By his own might to get
The trav'ler's garment off him.
   And it was settled thus
With no more words or wrangle,
   Nor further heat nor fuss.

Wind first began the tussle;
   He twisted, whirled, and beat
With rain and icy torrents,
   With driving hail and sleet.
The fiercer and the harder
   The mighty blowings blew,
The trav'ler for protection
   His cloak the tighter drew
Around his beaten body.
   Wrapped close from knees to chin
He faced the windy buffets
   That tried to wiggle in.
In vain the angry torrents;
   In vain each freezing blast;
Wind could not get that cloak off,
   So, gave it up at last.

Then, forth the Sun came shining,
　　Dispelling cold and mist
With warmth direct and kindly
　　That nothing could resist.
He sent his healing comfort
　　And all his gentle glow
Upon the weather-beaten
　　And wind-tossed man below.
No noise of strength or boasting,
　　No threatening word he spoke.
Soon, with a sigh of pleasure
　　Off came the trav'ler's cloak.

MORAL

Said Sun to Wind, "Good Neighbor,
　　Excuse me if I say,
'Tween *force* and wise *persuasion,*
　　Select the *gentler* way.
Calm wisdom is the stronger,
　　The surest and the best;
It lives and lasts the longer—
　　And *kindness* does the rest."

THE WAY TO LIVE

MAKE the best of everything
　　That happens every day.
Make the best of every one
　　You meet along the way.
　Hope the best for your own self.
　　Give all you have to give
Straight from the very best of you.
　　Yes, that's the way to live.

The DOG and his SHADOW

ONE day a very naughty dog
   Thought he would have a treat,
So, from the butcher's boy, he stole
   Two pounds or so of meat.

Then off he trotted hurriedly
   Across the field to find
A quiet place where he might eat
   In perfect peace of mind.

At last he trotted on a bridge
   That crossed a little brook.
The brook was laughing merrily,
   So doggie stopped to look.

That doggie was a thieving dog,
   And thieving dogs like that
Are apt to look around to see
   What brooks are laughing at.

His stolen piece of meat was held
   Between his guilty teeth,
As that bad dog looked down and snarled
   At little brook beneath.

He growled once and then some more.
   His snarly face was grim,
For there, beneath his very nose,
   A bad dog glared at him!

That other dog was bad as he,
  And it was no relief
For *our* bad dog to notice that
  The *other* was a thief.

For he, too, gripped between his teeth
  A monstrous piece of meat
Which looked much bigger than his own
  And forty times as sweet.

Now our bad dog grew jealous of
  The *other* thieving chap,
So, at the bigger piece of meat,
  Our doggie gave a snap.

Of course, by snapping so, he lost
  His piece of meat, which took
A journey to the bottom of
  The merry little brook.

And all *he* got by snapping so
  Was what such doggies get—
A merry sp*lash* from little brook
  That made him very wet.

Then little brook with laughter shook
  Until it almost cried,
And then it said,—"A greedy dog
  Is never satisfied.

"And as for thieves, they come to grief,
  So I would rather be
A little brook, quite satisfied
  With what *belongs* to me."

The
REED
and the
OAK
A Fable from
Aesop

ONE day an Oak Tree scorned a slender Reed.
  "Weak little thing," said he. "We brave Oak Trees
    Stand stiff and straight to meet the storm, while you
Bend down before the little passing breeze.
Ho! stand and face the storm by strength of limb.
Let might save all in times of stress or need.
I do not bend; I never yield like you,
O silly Reed!"

The Oak Tree hurt the feelings of the Reed.
With shame she trembled, but she answered naught.
That night a great storm came and all night long
The Oak in his unyielding manner fought.
But little Reed lay low before the storm,
And when the Sun of next bright morning woke
There stood the slender Reed unhurt beside
                    The fallen Oak.

The slender Reed then trembled as she said,
"It is not always stubbornness and might
Nor strength of will, nor fierce resistance that
Endures the storm or wins the savage fight.
It's often gentle yielding, without forceful deed
That wins us peace; *I* have the wisdom of
                    The slender Reed."

"WELL, let us race," said Tortoise quietly.
 "The prize five pounds-for five miles let it be.
And, if you will most heartily agree,
 Let Reynard Fox serve as the referee."

The HARE and the TORTOISE
A Fable from Aesop

THERE was a hare—a braggart hare was she,
    As full of boasts as forty hares might be.
    One day she met Old Tortoise as he went
In his slow way, on his own business bent.

With scornful kicks and friskings of her heels,
    She tried to show how speedy feeling feels;
And furthermore, insulted Tortoise for
    His slowness which all speedy hares abhor.

"Well, let us race," said Tortoise quietly.
    "The prize five pounds—for five miles let it be.
And, if you will most heartily agree,
    Let Reynard Fox serve as the referee."

The hare, with sniffs and very scornful smiles,
    Said, "Humph! Slow Poke, why not a *hundred* miles?
But five will do to prove my strength and speed."
    Thus on a race this funny pair agreed.

Off went the two: Hare like the very wind,
    With Tortoise plodding steadily behind.
In *steady going* he put all his trust
    While Hare in haste stirred up a lot of dust.

So fast that active, boastful rabbit sped,
　　Ere long she was at least two miles ahead;
So great the distance being in between
　　The two, no sign of Tortoise could be seen.

"Ha!" puffed the hare, "where is the lazy chap?
　　I've time, I think, to take a cozy nap.
A stretch of many hours there must be
　　Ere that Old Pokey catches up with me."

So, on the soft and cooling grass he lay
　　And slept a lot of precious time away;
While Tortoise, ever plodding, plodding on
　　With time to spare the long race fairly won.

MORAL

"Yes," said the Fox, "Dear Friends, I hardly need
　　To give a talk on boastful waste of speed;
Nor will I dwell upon the foolish waste
　　Of misdirected strength and wearing haste.
We are more sure to win a happy goal
　　And realize ambitions, on the whole,
By going, *going* ever straight ahead.
　　The swift in pride are very oft misled
By boasts too great and over-confidence,
　　And disrespect for others' powers; hence,
Their purses shrink and private feelings bleed
　　When *steady plodding* triumphs over *speed*."

The FOX and the CROW
A Fable from Aesop

OLD Lady Crow was very fond
  Of folly and of ease,
  But most especially she loved
A hunk of tasty cheese.
Not having any cash at hand
  (At least she'd not reveal it),
Or knowing how to *beg* for cheese,
  Dame Crow said she would *steal it.*

Forth to a near-by cot she flew.
  Upon a window-sill
Reposed a piece of cheese, and she
  Just nipped it in her bill.
She thought she was a clever crow:
  I think she was a *bad* one;
And I can safely prophesy
  Her end will be a sad one.
Away she flew and croaked in glee
  With her ill-gotten plunder;
And all she croaked about herself
  Makes *honest* children wonder.

"I'm very clever," chuckled she,
    Perched high up in a tree.
"At getting cheese with perfect ease
    No one can equal me.
I am a *marvel*, yes, I am.
    The cleverest of crows,
And I don't care a cheerful croak
    If everybody knows."
With vanity and swelling pride
    She took her chuckling fill,
The cheese held tight and proudly in
    Her *pec*-u-lating bill.

Just then a fox came walking by
    (A sly, old fox was he);
And, looking up, saw Madame Crow
    Perched high up in her tree.
But little cared Dame Crow as she
    Observed that fox beneath,
For she was safe so far above
    His sharp and shining teeth.
She therefore winked one yellow eye,
    And held on to her cheese,
And thought,—"I'm glad that foxes aren't
    Experts at climbing trees."

"Good morning, Madame," said the fox,
    In manner very sprightly;
Then, bowing low to Madame Crow,
    Continued most politely,—
"Oh, Madame, *how* the morning sun
    Shines on your wings and features.
You are indeed most *beau*-tiful,
    The loveliest of creatures!

No bird in all the world is half
    So strong, and swift, and wise;
None with such grace, and no one with
    Such *fascinating* eyes!
Your *voice* must be as wonderful
    As all your other parts,
I'm certain that the *songs you sing*
    Would captivate our hearts!"

All this most foxy flattery
    I hardly need to tell
Quite turned her head and from her perch
    She very nearly fell.
You see, when foxy flatterers
    With flattery get busy,
Vain crows, and those with foolish pride
    Are likely to get dizzy.
"I *have* a perfect voice," thought she,
    "And all the world will love it.
Yes, I will sing for Mr. Fox
    And positively prove it."

Then Dame Crow opened up her bill,
    According to the law
Of proper song and forth there came
    A most discordant—C - A - W!
Down fell the tasty hunk of cheese
    Between sly fox's paws
And in a moment it was lost
    Beyond that beastie's jaws.

Yes, cheese, like opportunity,
　From prideful persons slips;
Then scheming, foxy flatterers
　Just lick their naughty lips.
Off trotted crafty Mr. Fox.
　Dame Crow but hung her head
In foolish shame and this is what
　That fox with chuckles said,—

MORAL

"Ha, ha! Ho, Ho! You silly crow,
　'Tis very plain to see
That *wisdom* leaves the head and heart
　When in comes *vanity*.
Had you been satisfied to keep
　Your noisy croaking still,
You yet might have the cheese you **stole**
　Tucked safely in your bill.
But you let vanity deceive,
　And flattery undo you.
I hope this loss of stolen cheese
　Will be a lesson to you."

The FOX and the STORK
A Fable from Aesop

A BEASTIE sly was Reynard Fox,
  Sharp was his crafty nose—
A nose so made to suit his kind
 By Nature, I suppose.
But let that be as Nature bids,
 A fox most surely is
Quite justly credited with guile
 And slyness such as his.
Besides his slyness and his guile
 And other traits like these
He had a streak of *cruelty*
 Which made him love to *tease.*

Dr. Stork

One day, when rather bored with things,
 He thought of Doctor Stork,
A person more inclined to *think*
 Than waste good time in talk.
"He's said to be exceeding wise,"
 Thought Fox. "Well I will see
If Doctor Stork with all his brains
 Can get ahead of me.

Yes, I shall ask old Sobersides
 If he will come to dine.
I need a little practice in
 A favorite trick of mine."

That very day, Fox called on Stork.
  With manners *over*-fine,
He asked with foxy courtesy
  Old Doctor Stork to dine.
The stork was very much impressed
  By manners so polite,
So he accepted with grave thanks
  And quite an appetite.

Next day the fox, with crafty smiles
  And bows most grand and able,
Led Doctor Stork—that wise old bird—
  Straight to the dining table.
For such attention, Doctor Stork
  Expressed his gratitude;
Not for a moment thinking that
  His host was mean or rude.
Soup was provided for his guest,
  Served in a platter *flat;*
Now how could Stork with his thin bill
  Eat from a dish like that?
In vain he pecked into the soup,
  Which being liquid is
Extremely difficult to hold
  In such a bill as his.

So, hungrier and hungrier
  Old Stork grew every minute,
As Fox lapped from his shallow plate
  And left no liquid in it.
And as he lapped he chuckled, too,
  And licked his precious nose.
Without a word of just complaint
  Old Doctor Stork arose
And said, "I thank you, gentle host!
  I promise to repay
With interest, the courtesy
  You've shown to me to-day."

Old Stork went home to mediate,
  Then with a *bilious* smile
Exclaimed, "I'll give that crafty fox
  A taste of his own guile!"
So then one day quite formally
  He cordially invited
That fox to dine. Fox said that he
  Was very much delighted.
The feast set out for Mr. Fox
  Was fit for kings to eat.
'Twas mince-meat, very savory,
  A most inviting treat.
And here is where the fun begins,
  The meal was served within
A *tall glass jar* that had a neck
  Extremely *long and thin.*
"Please help yourself," said Doctor Stork.
  "I pray you eat your fill!"
As down into the vase *he* thrust
  His long, convenient bill.

Thus Doctor Stork outwitted Fox,
  Who slyly hung his head,
And to conceal his feelings rose
  And most politely said:
"A clever joke I'm bound to say.
  A lesson you have taught me.
I must acknowledge, Doctor Stork,
  You certainly have caught me."
With no more words or further bows
  That tricky fox departed,
Mayhap, not cured of foxiness,
  But certainly downhearted.

MORAL

The moral to this fable is
  With little trouble guessed,
And is in Reynard's very words
  Most suitably expressed:—
"Some get their soup with tongues that lap;
  Stork by a bill that picks.
Next time I'll measure *noses* when
  I play my foxy tricks.
In other words, it's just as well
  In reckoning our powers
To learn that *other* fellows' gifts
  May fully equal ours."

SUNSHINE

THE days are full of light and sun
    With just a little rain,
But all the days bring many things
    To make them bright again.

Sometimes the clouds fill up the sky
    And hide the sun awhile,
But by and by the sun comes out
    With all the brighter smile.

Sometimes our hearts are like the days
    With sun and clouds and rain;
Our bodies feel at times the touch
    Of sickness or of pain.

But let us all remember *this*—
    God's sun is yours and mine;
Behind our rain and clouds and pain
    We know *it has to shine.*

The LION and the MOUSE
A Fable from Aesop

A TIRED lion, after hunting lay
    Asleep beneath a great and shady tree.
    Then ran a mouse across his back and he
Awoke with anger and abused dismay.
In rage he rose and caught his tiny prey
    Beneath his paw. "Have mercy, Sire!" cried she,
    "You are too *big* to kill poor *little* me."
"Quite true," said he, and let her run away.

One day he roamed that very neighborhood.
    A monarch of all beasts he was and yet
He hunted all alone in search of food;
    And no one warned him that a trap was set
To catch him as he wandered in the wood.
    So he, poor beast, soon fell into the net.

Oh, how he struggled with all might and main
    To free himself. With angry rend and roar
    Upon the cruel net he bit and tore,
But all his frantic struggle was in vain.
The little mouse heard lion's roars of pain
    And hurried up to pay a grateful score.
    Said she, "I pray don't struggle any more
And you shall have your freedom once again."

With no more words she nibbled at the net,
    And presently the monarch beast was free.
The tiny mouse had fully paid her debt.
    "Ah," lion said, "most truly wise are we,
If in our strength we never once forget
    How *great* the might of *littleness* can be."

STRENGTH

THE strong and great should not be proud
    And laugh at those who may be weak,
For who can tell but they may give,
    In time of need, the help we seek.

We may be little, but perhaps
    We have the energy and skill
To do what bigness cannot do
    With all its strength and boastful will.

We may be big and strong and grand,
    Perhaps too big to clearly see
The hidden strength in little things
    Or just how wise the small may be.

THE COCK and the FOX
A Fable from Aesop

ONE early morn old Mr. Cock
    Flew up an apple tree.
    He crowed with all his might and main,
For *grand* at crows was he.
The sun was rising in the sky,
    The grass was bright with dew;
So, Mr. Cock with joyful pride
    Called, *"Cock-a-doodle-doo."*

Along came Mr. Reynard Fox
    And promptly noticed him;
But he regretted that the Cock
    Sat on so high a limb.

"Good morning, Sir," said Mr. Fox,
    "I have the *greatest* news!"
"You have?" replied the wise old Cock,
    "Then tell me if you choose.
Oh, by the way, how do you like
    My *cock-a-doodle-doos?*"

"Come down," said crafty **Mr. Fox**;
   But wise old rooster knew
When he was safe, and all he said
   Was *"Cock-a-doodle-doo!"*
"The news," quoth Fox, "is that the birds
   And beasts have all made peace.
No longer will they kill or hunt;
   All horrid war must cease.
From this day forth true brotherhood
   Shall rule the forests wide.
Like trusting friends, we all will live
   And prosper side by side.
Just look at me and you'll agree
   You have no grounds to doubt it,
Hop down beside me and I'll tell
   A good deal more about it."

But rooster winked his wise old eye
   And cocked a little ear;
Then said, "Now can it really be
   The hunter's horn I hear?"

"What do you say you think you hear?"
   Said Reynard, most politely.
"Oh, nothing but the hunter's horn,
   If I am hearing rightly;
And come to think of it a bit,
   There are some other sounds
That seem to me quite strangely like
   A pack of baying hounds."

With not so much as "Good-bye, Sir,"
   That sly Fox then departed;
And by the look of his long tail
   He must have been downhearted.

"Why such a hurry?" cried the Cock.
　"Oh, maybe I was *wrong*
About the peace of which I spoke;
　I think I'll trot along."

'Twas easy for old Cock to judge
　By Fox's observation
That he was somewhat disinclined
　To further conversation.

"Ha," chuckled wise old Mr. Cock,
　"Our doubts of mind increase
When politicians like that Fox
　Talk brotherhood and peace!"

Moral:

An early morning smile should show
　The joy of friendly meetings.
Our "How-de-do's" should ever be
　The most unselfish greetings.
The smirky smile that covers guile
　With dignity, beware of.
When giving friendliness be sure
　It is well taken care of.
When quarrelers talk much of *peace,*
　And foxes grin at you, Dear,
Just wink a merry eye and say,—
　"Oh, *'cock-a-doodle-doo,'* Dear."

The VAIN JACKDAW
A Fable from Aesop

ONE day a jackdaw walked around
The pleasant garden paths and found
Some peacock feathers on the ground.
"Ha, ha! He, hum!" with squawks said he,
"Most useful will these feathers be
To make a peacock bird of me,
And fool my common family."

He was a very foolish bird,
And called his kind the "common herd."
His vanity was quite absurd.
To get into the social swim
He started in at once to trim
Those feathers to the end of him.
(Oh, what a very silly stroke!
The cast-off clothes of grander folk!
But jackdaw didn't see the joke.)
Said he, "I'll have a peacock's tail;
Such dress and beauty cannot fail
In social matters to prevail,
And give a worthy place to me
In all the best society."

So jackdaw stuck the feathers to
The place where *his* tail feathers grew,
Then stretched his neck to take a view
Of his unfitting finery.
A shallow-pated bird was he
As any one of sense could see.

He turned his back upon the daws
With haughty head and spreading claws,
Defying Nature's goodly laws.
He was just *stuffed* with pride and so
He strutted forth to Peacock Row,
Convinced he made a pretty show;
And furthermore, that bird believed
He had the peacocks all deceived,
And every social hope achieved.

But peacocks are not slow to find
A dressy difference 'tween their kind
And those of other tastes of mind
(Especially feathers worn behind),
So what could any one expect
From peacock circles so select?
That silly daw, so grandly decked,
Was pushed and pulled, rebuffed and pecked,
Until he was completely *wrecked*.

On humbled manners sadly bent,
Ashamed of *shame,* that jackdaw went
To join his friends in hopes that they
Had failed to see the foolish way
His common sense had gone astray.
But they, remembering that he
Had scorned his own dear family,
Said to him then: "Be off with thee,
We can't endure thy vanity!
Be off and learn to be content
With what ye are and Nature meant
A daw to be. And then repent
Thy sins of foolish snobbery.
And other ones of vanity.
Don't try to be what ye are not,
Plucked by thy betters and a blot
Despised by equals—so just *trot!*"

MORAL

With but few words we now are able
To give the moral of this fable;
So here are those familiar words—
"Fine feathers do not make fine birds."

LITTLE SMILES

WHEN my heart's a little sore,
    And 'most everything's a bore,
And nothing that I try is quite worth **while;**
    When I can't see any fun
In myself or any one,
      Then it's time for me to smile a
                  Little Smile.

When I'm out of sorts and blue
    When I don't know what to do,
When my playthings are a cluttered, mussy **pile;**
    When dear Mother cannot see
What is wrong with her and me,
      Then it's time for me to smile a
                  Little Smile.

If I smile a little smile,
    In a very little while
I will drive away my mully-grubs and trials.
    Yes, I think I'll have a face
That's a very pleasant place,
      Just because it's always full of
                  Little Smiles.

The GOOSE that laid the GOLDEN EGGS
A Fable from Aesop

ONCE on a time there was a man—
  A greedy person who
Was mean in every sort of way
  And avaricious, too,
The more he got, the less he gave,
  And stingier he grew.

This undeserving man possessed
  A goose who used to lay
With uncomplaining willingness
  A golden egg each day.
No thanks she got for all her pains,
  And not a penny's pay.

But her mean owner, not content
  With all his golden store
(Not even when he counted up
  The gold eggs by the score),
Grew greedier and greedier
  Because he hadn't more.

So, one sad day the miser said,
  "I'll kill that goose and see
How many eggs she has inside.
  A worthless goose is she!
If she can't lay more eggs a day,
  She is no use to me."

And so he killed "The Golden Goose"
  With greedy, cruel pleasure,
And looked inside of her to find
  A lot of golden treasure.
But that man's disappointment was
  Beyond all thought or measure.

MORAL

Of course, he found no eggs at all. His dream of wealth was sped.
His greediness and discontent had given naught instead.
Good fortune was forever gone. *The Golden Goose was dead!*

THERE was a boy who tended sheep,
Upon a hillside green
Where fragrant clovers sweetly grew,
With cowslips in between.

WOLF! WOLF!
A Fable from Aesop

THERE was a boy who tended sheep,
   Upon a hillside green
    Where fragrant clovers sweetly grew,
With cowslips in between.
The sun was bright and everything
   Seemed happy and serene.

But sometimes things are otherwise
   Than seemingly appear,
For wolves attacked the shepherd's flocks
   From forests lying near.
And often slew the sheep and filled
   The folk with cruel fear.

But this same shepherd boy was stuffed
   With mischief to the eyes,
Which very, very often leads
   To mischief-making lies,
As well as other wickedness
   That proper folk despise.

One day when all was going well
  And not a wolf in sight,
When he and all the sheep were safe,
  And everything was right,
He cried, *"Wolf! Wolf!"* most lustily
  As if in awful fright.

Up hastened toilers from the field,
  And friends from hut and hall;
They rushed to save him from the wolves
  In answer to his call;
When they arrived upon the scene
  There were no wolves at all.

And what is worse, this boy whose mind
  Worked in this foolish vein
Played that same trick a *lot* of times.
  This made his friends complain
And say, "We won't *believe* him if
  He calls, 'Wolf! Wolf!' again."

But wolves one day did *really* come!
   "Wolf! Wolf! Come help!" he cried,
But all his friends, remembering
   How often he had lied,
Paid no attention to his calls,
   And so that shepherd died!

MORAL

The moral to this fable is
   A very simple one:
We should not ever tell a lie,
   Not even *"just for fun."*
For lies of any kind weave harm
   That cannot be undone.
And as for jokes called "practical,"
   On friends or other folk,
These are the *meanest* kind of fun;
   They almost always cloak
A cruel heart, and in the end
   Just punishment provoke.

TRUTH IS BEST

SIMPLE TRUTH

WE always tell the simple Truth;
  We do so, for we love it.
There's nothing strong, nor big enough
  To get the better of it.

A lie is like a shadow, or
  A wordy, windy bubble;
It holds no good, it has no use,
  It brings us only trouble.

The Truth is like a golden robe,
  That honors those who wear it,
Its beauty never shall be spoiled;
  No lie shall soil or tear it.

LIFE
and LIVING

A LITTLE Smile is well worth while,
   A merry Laugh is sweeter,
A kindly Deed in time of need
   Makes Happiness completer.
A lot of Fun when Work is done,
   A deal of thoughtful Giving,
Friends good as gold to have and hold—
   All this is Life and Living.

The MISER
A Fable from Aesop

THERE was a miser, shrivelled, hard, and cold,
Who went each day to count his buried gold.
This hoard was tied up in a bag and he
Dug a deep hole beneath a spreading tree
And hid it there.

There was a peasant who
Had watched his frequent journeys and he knew
There must be reasons why that miser went
With sneaking steps upon some secret bent.
And so that person followed him one day
And saw just where the miser's treasure lay.
He waited for his chance, then promptly stole
The bag of treasure from the secret hole.

That very day, discovering his loss,
The miser was in agonies, of course,
He raged about and tore his scanty hair,
Crying aloud in desperate despair.
(But we don't sympathize, I must confess.)

A passer-by, observing his distress,
Asked him the cause; and then the miser told
How he had lost his buried bag of gold:
A villain *thief* had surely stolen it.
Thereat he had *another* raging fit.

MORAL

"Ah," said the stranger, "really, I can't see
Of what good use such *buried* gold can be.
Your treasure brought you neither joy nor good,
So why not hide a stone or log of wood
Down in the empty hole, and then pretend
It is the gold you never give nor spend?
Yes, yes, a stone will serve you quite as well,
And may be even better—who can tell?"

The MICE in COUNCIL
A Fable from Aesop

A BAND of mice lived in a house,
  Where they most freely helped themselves
    Just as they would
    (And really could)
To everything on pantry shelves.

With very selfish appetites
They rummaged here and ravaged there,
    Most wretched blights
    On other's rights—
An awful nuisance, I declare.

So Lady Housewife got a cat,
A most successful mouser, too.
    With puss about
    No mouse came out.
What were the ravagers to do?

That cat went stalking everywhere
With habits dangerous and rude.
    Why, every mouse
    In that same house
Would starve to death for want of food!

So, in their trouble deep and dark,
They called a meeting of the mice
    To have a chat
    On pussy cat
In hopes of gaining good advice.

So they discussed their troubles much
From every point and awkward angle.
    They got some nice
    And strange advice
But none to straighten out the tangle.

At last a young, conceited mouse
Arose and made this little chat:
    "Dear friends, I know
    And I will show
A way to fool that cruel cat.

Now, I propose we hang a bell
About her neck; then, by its sound
    All mice will hear
    Its tinkle clear
When she is anywhere around."

Then he sat down 'mid great applause.
Most sage remarks! A noble cause!
    Such good advice
    For starving mice!
Such clappings of those tiny claws!

But presently an *ancient* mouse,
Who had not said a word before,
    Rose quietly;
    And thus spake he
When formally allowed "the floor."

"I think the plan is excellent,
And doubtless our young speaker can
    In few words say
    What is the way
To carry out his clever plan.

In other words, it isn't plain
To me and other persons that
    We want to choose
    The hero who's
To be the one *to bell the cat!*"

MORAL

Conceited folks are apt to be
Quick to advise with thoughtless chatter.
    But how to *do*
    And put things through
Is really quite another matter.

A NEW DAY

 NEW day is begun;
   Before our watching eyes,
Bright in the golden sun
   A day of goodness lies.

The joys of yesterday
   Live doubly sweet again,
But wrong is far away
   And gone are fear and pain.

Our happy *now* is bright,
   Plain is the sunlit way.
Past is the shadowed night;
   Good is our new To-day.

Now let our hearts go out
   Rejoicing; let us say,
"We need not fear nor doubt,
   For this is God's New Day."

The CROW and the PITCHER
A Fable from Aesop

A CROW whose throat was dry with thirst
    Beheld a pitcher near;
    He flew to it in great delight
And gratitude sincere.

Into the pitcher then he looked,
    Perched firmly up above it;
Yes, there was water, but indeed
    A very little of it.

And then, the water was, alas,
    All at the *bottom,* too.
He could not reach a drop of it;
    So what was he to do?

He tried to move the pitcher and
    With push and pull and puff
He worked to turn it over but
    He was not strong enough.

Crow did not whine at this hard luck,
    Nor did he even get
The least impatient as he said,—
    "I'll solve the problem yet!

"We *do* knock down all obstacles
  By giving them no quarter.
I *can* find out an easy way
  To get my drink of water."

Crow thought things out most quietly
  And then he looked around
And saw a lot of pebbles which
  Were scattered on the ground.

"Just what I want!" said Mr. Crow.
  He put them one by one
Into the pitcher 'til at last
  The victory was won.

Of course the sinking pebbles pushed
  The water up and up,
So he could drink as easily
  As from a shallow cup.

MORAL

The moral, or the lesson of
  This simple fable is—
That he who knows he knows he *can*
  Is he who *able* is.
In other words, if we but *know*
  The magic power in
The words, *"I CAN,"* there is no goal
  This *magic* cannot win.

PATIENCE

PATIENCE is the heart of wisdom.
  Patience makes the spirit strong.
Patience sees beyond the shadows
  Into sunshine, smiles and song.
Patience long and patience loving
  Is the love of God within us.
There is nothing great and goodly
  Loving patience cannot win us.

The CAT and the MICE ~
A Fable from Aesop

THERE was a house quite overrun
    With many hungry mice.
       And so the farmer's lady took
  Some neighborly advice.
She got a cat whose appetite
    Of mercy was bereft;
The cat chased lots of mice away,
    And ate them, right and left.

Observing this, the last few mice
    On preservation bent,
Got very busy and they called
    A mousekind parliament.
They promptly made a certain law
    To save their little selves—
"No mouse should ever go below
    The upper pantry shelves."

The law worked well as you shall see;
  Puss said in rage, "Oh, drat them!
How do the silly things expect
  A fellow to get at them?
I'll have to think the matter out.
  Ah, ha, it has been said
That mice aren't scared of cats if they
  Look really *good and dead.*"

So kit cat hung himself up high
  On two strong wooden pegs;
He managed *it* so that he should hang
  By his two "hinder" legs.
He was as limp as limp could be
  From tail down to his head,
And otherwise he made himself
  Look *oh so "good and dead."*

But these wise mice on *upper* shelves
    Were not deceived at all,
For they knew that a *living* cat
    Hung there against the wall.
And one old mouse (a sly old mouse),
    Popped forth his ancient head
And in the most sarcastic tones
    With jiggling whiskers said—

"Your *wits* are also upside down,
    If you imagine that
We trust a living, or a dead,
    Or *any* kind of cat.
A cat's a *cat,* here, there, and at,
    Eye, tooth and tearing claw.
We would not trust you even if
    Your skin were stuffed with straw.

MORAL

Once suffering from hungry cats
    We wisely shun and dread, Sir,
A cat in any form at all,
    Alive, or *'good and dead'* Sir."

Au revoir dear little Friends!
Here Your Book of Fables
ENDS

THE heart is wiser than the head; But, let's by both be always led.